The Four Bodies of Being

Mapping your Energy Bodies-the where, why, and how of your physical, astral, mental and soul body placement.

Patsy Stanley

PB ISBN 9798993585628

The Four Bodies

Discovering the Energy Maps of Who You Are

Your Conscious Awareness:

Your conscious awareness is seated in your manifested physical body in this physical realm. That's where it is seated. Because we all have to have an energy body-the physical body- that is a match to the Earth's laws and energies as well as a match to the universe, since we are made of star material, too.

Our physical body falls in line with the Laws of Manifestation as any vehicle has to. All are different and all progress forward from the One and obey the Law.

In order to manifest into the physical- and to be awarded a physical body to operate through, we must agree to go through two Earth initiations.

The Two Earth Initiations

The two initiations that take place when one is manifesting onto a planet:

Birth- It is the first initiation one receives upon arrival, and Death-is the last initiation one receives upon leaving a planet.

Both initiations are contracts/holy covenants you must commit to with the planet about how your consciousness is going to Manifest into Matter on that planet. That includes how, why, where, and how long you will be using that body/ Form.

The first Earth initiation takes place at birth. Here is the process. When you are born, in that first moment of breath, you are taking in the Earth Element. The Earth Elements are the energies of solidarity. You become solid. You are in Matter. Consciousness residing in Matter. Your Intentions and reasons for desiring to manifest into Form have formed you. It has happened.

The Earth element has grounded you and connected you to the planet. This is the energy through which the silver cord from the astral plane becomes connected to the solar plexus. You take your first breath of life, and the energy in your **physica**l umbilical cord is separated from your mother. Earth takes over.

At the same time, the silver umbilical between you and your mother's emotional bodies become permanently connected and your other bodies, emotional, mental, and lower soul, connect to the astral body.

The soul incarnates, allowing the life force to infuse into the physical. Who you really are could not incarnate until that moment of birth, until that process took place.

The second Earth initiation is death. When you leave a planet, you must leave what belongs to that planet behind. It is in the orderly progression of Matter to leave your physical body behind when leaving Earth.

Your Matter was put out on loan, with a contract between you and that planet, and has to be returned in either long term installments, or within a short time. This basic foundation underlies all of the journeys the consciousness of all Matter carries into the different worlds we visit.

Both Birth and Death are transformations. Transformations are processes, because energy does not die. Energy just changes its form, time after time.

These two initiations allow us to have the experience of the five sensory perceptions that are available to us on Earth through donning a physical body.

Death is the last initiation one receives in the journey homeward each lifetime. This process is expressed through the blending of the Higher and Lower natures of that consciousness.

All elimination and assimilation processes are made possible through these two planet Earth Initiations.

However, it doesn't stop with the personal part. We not only agree to the Birth and Death initiations on planet Earth, we agree to help Earth with its own energy processes and growth. Since we're made of the same star material Earth is made of, it's a go.

Depending on when we show up here and how, we agree to join soul groups that are processing Earth energies at that time.

We live and die in soul groups. We have to participate in Earth life events. Earth is the huge living being we live on. And Earth, like other planets, has its ups and downs. It has different ages it lives through.

Then there are the bigger events Earth goes through, like the issues that arise approximately every 13,000 years when it turns the corner of its elliptical path, when humans have to help Earth shift its polarity to the opposite polarity it has been in. That's the matriarchy-patriarchy stuff.

The Four Bodies:
Physical
Astral/emotional
Mental
Lower Soul

The Physical Body:

The physical body experiences and expresses the energies working on the physical plane of existence. The other three bodies are grounded within the physical body which has the densest/slowest energy vibration. The physical body provides a point in "now" time. It provides all four bodies a relationship with Earth. The physical body is the passport or identity that allows us to reside in this reality. That is the definition of a "Vehicle". All four bodies are vehicles for different parts of your experiencing and expressing during your lifetime. Three can't be seen. One can.

That is because the other three bodies/vehicles reside in higher levels of vibration/faster moving energies- that cannot be seen in the realm of physical reality. Each of the three bodies experience and express their life in this reality in their own specific ways through their attachment to the vehicle/physical body.

The physical body has its own life force. It has integrity and feelings and it is psychic in its own right.

The energies on the physical plane vibrate up to 186,000 m.p.h., at which point the faster and higher emotional/astral planes vibrations begin. Above the astral planes lie the mental planes, which are even faster, then the soul planes, fastest of the four lower bodies of humankind.

The five senses in the physical body, or vehicle, are also present in all of the bodies.

Energy moves down into the physical, therefore, the physical body reflects what your other bodies are up to, their activities and principles.

The Astral Body

Most everybody has many teachers on the astral planes, but very few realize this and ask for their help.

We experience and express our feeling nature through our astral body and its energy planes. It is the vehicle for experiencing and expressing our emotions. Our feelings about everything is seated in the astral body. Everything that has ever been felt, exists somewhere on the astral planes.

The astral plane interpenetrates and vivifies the physical body with the life force.

Everything that exists on the physical plane, exists on the astral plane, and a whole bunch more.

All energies move from the inner to the outer. For anything to manifest, it must have first existed at a minimum, on the astral plane. The astral plane is the first cause of manifestation. The astral body has tremendous power over what takes place in our physical life.

The imagination that each human carries is very powerful, and it resides on the astral plane. The imagination pulls in the energies, shapes them through fantasy and imagination. Life is given to those energies by the level of desire emitted by the person. Whatever you are feeling, wanting, desiring, imagining, on the astral plane, will manifest. You may not know when or where, but it will take place.

One of the major levels of the power of cause and effect resides in the astral body. This power resides within the emotional body- the child in you- that you carry around with you all of your life. That inner child is the vehicle through which you experience and learn about the levels of life that correspond to the astral plane of existence.

To take care of the child within, to take care of your emotional/astral body-means staying in touch with your wants, imagination, dreams, and desires. Most children are not taught by their parents to do this, and so the awareness of how to manage the power of this part of the self is not understood.

All day long, every day of your life, the astral body is filled with all kinds of information about your emotions. Keep in touch with it by asking yourself how you are feeling about the different parts of life you come in contact with every day. Divide them up, pay attention, and solve.

When the astral body wants to create something, it reaches both up and down to the energies of the lower physical and higher mental bodies to get it done. They work together through the power of the desire of the astral body to get it done.

No one else can take care of your astral body for you. Your energy is specific to it. Taking care of it means having your needs met. It means having your dreams, desires, and imagination manifest through your creativity. You have a choice about whether to pay attention to what you are feeling or not. To the degree that that pay attention and learn emotional regulation and emotional intelligence, you will stay young in a timeless way, and alive to the wonders of the world you live in.

The emotional patterning that your mother and father gave you is habit patterning that always shows up on the astral planes. This patterning affects what you do to take care of that part of you. You are in choice about whether the emotional patterning you received from Mother and Father is still enough for you and still works for you. It is good to throw out the parts that no longer work, they don't fit your world today, and to explore new connections and feelings.

You are responsible for your feeling nature and what it is doing. You alone are the parent of the child within yourself. It's your DNA, baby! After you grow up, you are responsible for not allowing that child to get beat up. Protect it. Learn to ask for what you want. You may get told no a lot, but if it is what you really want, then keep on asking until you help your child find a way to have it.

Listen to your inner child and respect what it has to say. Pay attention to it. Tell your inner child the truth. Don't make promises you can't keep! That child within you is not a stranger. It has been with you twenty four hours a day, all of your life. It probably has plenty to tell you about how you have treated it when you connect with it. So ask and listen and learn. It actually becomes quite delightful!

Don't think that the child within is a small, ineffective part of yourself that you can ignore, or that you left behind with childhood. That's B.S. The inner child that lives within each of us is the HEART of the blessed whole self. Because it is so powerful, without it, our dreams cannot come true. Your imagination can wither away. Your wants, needs, and deepest desires cannot come true throughout any of the four bodies without the astral body's willing participation.

The astral body is the vehicle through which we FEEL about spirituality. Energy blocks cannot be removed without its help. Life cannot flow without its help. The electro-magnetic fluids throughout all the bodies are balanced through the astral/emotional bodies experiences in life. Emotions ride the endocrine system to where they need to go.

 Get in touch with this part of yourself. Learn to parent it. Listen and talk to the child within you. Give it what it needs that you know how to do, and find a place to learn to give it what you didn't get emotionally, and needed when you were a child.

The degree to which we connect, nourish and understand the child within ourselves, is the degree to which we can take emotional responsibility for the aspects of the life we are living.

The degree of connection and creativity in your life comes directly from the connection to the astral body.

For the astral body is the heart of man kinds desires, hopes, wishes, imagination, and all of the feeling nature's manifestations and structures that correspond to the emotional energies of life. It doesn't think, formulate ideas, has no concepts, and doesn't "know" anything. Don't let that fool you into thinking it is not powerful.

The astral, or emotional, body, interpenetrates and vivifies the physical body. Whatever manifests into the physical, has to pass through the astral planes of energy. This means that the astral body is highly important to understand and connect with, because it has tremendous power over what is going to take place in your physical life.

The astral body maintains the balance of the electro-magnetic fluids throughout all of the bodies. The electro-magnetic fluids of life stay balanced through the emotions each individual part of life carries, and, all parts of life carry emotions that need to be tended to. It can become quite a juggling act, especially when we feel so many different ways about a particular thing. Time to call a board meeting!

In the physical body, the endocrine system is the major contact point for emotions to flow and process through. Access to energy comes through feelings. Paradoxes and the dance of life occur through emotional energy. The emotions are as valuable to us as gold is to the Earth.

The Mental body

The astral body is the heart of mankind.
The mental body is the mind of mankind.
The mind is the one that usually thinks it runs the show. (J.S.)

Mental bodies are the vehicles that experience/(fem.)and express/(Masc.) the energies that correspond to your thoughts, everyone else's thoughts, group thoughts, which are ideas, and groups of ideas which are concepts, and the higher aspects of the mind.

The higher aspect of the mind is the skeptic, (it says, how come? What I notice is…why?) It is the conscious observer of the process that is going on with you. It asks questions all of the time.

Mental energy is generally crisp and clear, and filled with thought provoking stuff. Mental energy operates on a higher level of vibration than the astral body does.

Between the astral body and the mental body, lies the lower causal planes of existence that correspond to the spiritual nature which envelops and literally becomes the causal level for all emotional experiencing. There are very few people who have a low causal body because it is developed very long into the evolutionary process. Read my book titled –The Mental Body for more information on the parts and practices of the mental body.

The Soul Body

The soul body is the vehicle of experience and expression for the energies of the soul. The soul planes have a positive or masculine polarity.

Thus we hear about the Light, not the Dark. "Moving into the light". "I know" are soul statements. Your soul energies correspond to universal life and its principles.

It is the part of you in training to understand and learn about thinking in terms of the similarities all life has, including humans, instead of the differences. Both similarities and differences are to be viewed in terms of good or bad. Or in any two dimensional thinking. They are both everywhere in life.

Your soul is the eternal student studying life, and its purpose is to come to know the truth for itself, and for all others.

It is through the soul body that we develop a more expanded way of thinking about life, and discover more about our destiny, or purpose on Earth, and begin to join with others in universal feelings and desires.

The soul of the self has to grow into becoming aware that time does not end; it becomes aware of eternal life. It may not know the details of how it all works, but it does know that to be the truth for itself. That realization changes every relationship in the life of that person.

The more you learn about yourself, the more realizations you have. At some point in the learning process, you realize that everyone else is working on their growth in their own way, and it is not up to you to interfere or judge them. This kind of tolerance comes from realizing that the way you were taught that things work, and the way they really work, are very different. That kind of realization, takes place in the soul body. The soul learns that:

All truth is self experienced knowledge. Every person is connected to everything in creation, and through this connection, they can come to understand what is happening with all others.

The soul learns that the big secret is that the more you know about yourself, the more you know about everyone else.

When you begin to realize that everyone is growing in their own way, at their own pace, then at that time, you realize that way that you have been taught, and the way it really works are two very different things.

A larger form of connection begins, for when the soul knows time is eternal, only then can it take the time it needs to operate from the new understanding.

Mates and all relationships begin to be redefined.

When you realize that you may have spent lifetimes knowing another person, and you might encounter them again in another life time, how you treat them now changes. Because it is going to have an impact on any future you might have together, your feelings towards them change.

The soul processes the energies of universal desires, universal thoughts, and universal needs. The soul speaks the language of intention. Soul awareness pays attention to what is happening on this planet. When we pick up a newspaper, or hear about another disaster on the planet, our soul processes our feelings about that event.

We are here to understand more of life. Everything we do has substance and meaning, and consequence. As the soul comes to know the truth for itself, it will stand in that truth, regardless of what anyone or whole groups of people say about it. The mind cannot be changed.

The soul has a job to do here. It needs to get to know itself. It needs to learn what the physical, astral, and mental bodies it is a part of, need in order to achieve connection. It is the soul that can do an overall comparison of life. The soul is the part of the self that has access to the collective unconscious, and to every thought that has ever been created.

Questions of fairness, integrity, loyalty, ethics, begin to be examined, with the purpose of assisting the soul to gain a better, more compassionate position through understanding the life it is experiencing.

The soul brings a person into a sense of connection with themselves. It is the higher way of feeling. Recognizing cruelty to another person on the soul level brings sadness, because the soul becomes more and more aware of the laws of karma. The soul knows that the energy that is put out is going to come back, and it does not want to be an instrument of pain.

The soul learns about ethics and loyalty, and fairness from a higher place that humanity has no language for. Souls have negative and positive polarities and feelings, and are in a learning process just as the other parts of the self are. As the soul wakes up, it begins the process of asking questions that are based on life as it needs to be lived in the highest good of all. Connection to the rest of the bodies it is a part of, begins to take place.

As soul awareness expands, the level of operation and vibration within your being, and the awareness you carry from lifetime to lifetime to increases. Realizations come from the inner self. Truth is self experienced knowledge. Knowing changes everything. When you experience the truth in your own life, you are able to stand in that truth, regardless of the degree of opposition.

During the individuation process of growth, we learned that we are not responsible for anyone else and how they feel. We just need to take care of ourselves. This is a necessary process that everyone must go through.

But there are higher laws. It is through the soul that we move past the individuation process, and learn about the connection of all of Life to itself.

It is said that you are not responsible for anyone else, that you need only look out for yourself. Except that there is a higher law that says that what is good for one part of God is good for all parts of God.

We live in a world that doesn't understand that there is a point to understanding life. Pursuing smaller truths lead to understanding bigger truths. Realizations. or the lack of them, serve to connect us with life, or to separate us from it. It is your right, and the work of the soul, to pursue a greater understanding of life, and to learn how connection truly works.

Everything we do has meaning, whether we understand it or not. Every action we take, has a consequence. What we focus on, we will come to understand. The body for getting to know the truth for yourself, is the soul body.

Now- All people have soul parts of themselves that are "gone" on purpose. The patterning for jumping into the spiritual realms to accomplish something we can- or can't possibly do, is given to us by our parents.

We genetically come from, and attempt this activity, in order to try to expand past our two dimensional thinking into sacred geometry.

We are trying to be a soul architect.

The Basic Polarities in the Four Bodies:

Energy requires polarization to exist. In the Beginning was the Word. And from the Word proceeded the Light and the Dark. The dual nature of the Light and the Dark are the dual, basic foundations of energy.

The interaction and stressors between these two polar opposites hold our reality in place.

This duality is both masculine and feminine.

They are governed by polarity and the pattern's that polarity carries- (quantum physics)

Some polarity patterns are:

Cause and effect

North and south Poles of magnet-1 pole is the principle of radiation and separation, out of which comes expansion and all forms of motion.

The other pole is the principle of fusion, out of which comes all forms of fusion, connection and matter.

Our physical mother and father represent this Dual Nature in our personal lives. The polarity stress between the two of them creates our personal patterns, genetics, and environment.

Everything works in pairs-fractal duality.

Duality on the different levels:

Physical

Emotional

Mental

Soul

Polarity = Duality –in the four bodies; When you are born you are polarized to gender and to being negative or positive emotionally.

Each human being has a "body" residing in each of the four basic energy vibration areas. Each of these body/areas has a polarity simply because it contains both-and different amounts of Matter/magnetic and Motion/electric. Thus, the energy calibrations are different for each of the four basic bodies of the self.

Throughout all esoteric literature and sacred teachings, the parts of the self are described as bodies. Each body that makes up the self, has its own energy vibration and reality/plane of existence that it resides on. Each body is connected to the other bodies.

Each level of energy, or plane of existence, and the body that resides therein, addresses growth in different ways.

Each body is an integral part of the self we are, and without it, the rest cannot survive. All of the planes of existence and the bodies that reside therein, work together to form who we are.

Interaction between the bodies has specific polarities to it.

Here is each body's polarity by the two genders:

Male gender polarity:

Physical-positive

Emotional/astral- negative

Mental- positive

Soul- negative

Female gender polarity:
Physical-negative
Emotional/astral-positive
Mental- negative
Soul-positive

Above the soul plane energies are the Spirit planes, where the energy is moving so fast that androgeny can occur. You are born with one or the other gender. Your gender does not and cannot change throughout your lifetime.

The polarities reverse all the way up through the four bodies and planes of existence. Each energy plane is subdivided into areas, but that information is for another book. But you get the idea. Each plane reverses so that there is a match for both positive and negative polarities in each gender, therefore balance equaling = electro-magnetism.

What does Polarity look like on the physical plane of existence?

Males have a positive polarity. That means they are more active, larger, and can do more physical labor them females. They do the strongest expression in all that can be seen physically. To men, giving love in the physical is positive. They want to give it to you, to share it with you, because it is positive, meaning good, to them. Women's role in physical love, to men, is to be receptive.(magnetic, or negative)

Females have a negative polarity. They are less active, smaller, and can do less physical labor than males on the physical plane. They are the receivers.

Polarity on the astral plane of existence:
Males have a negative polarity emotionally. They are the receivers. If women ask very much from men emotionally, on the astral planes, she's going to be identified with their mother's negative qualities very rapidly.

Because men are smaller, receptive and less active emotionally on the emotional planes, in love relationships, they avoid because they don't feel powerful there.

Females have a positive polarity emotionally. They are more active, larger, and can do more emotional work than males. They are the expressers. The astral context is feelings and emotions.

Men have typically been overwhelmed by women's energy emotionally. Just as many women feel bombarded by men on the physical plane, many men feel bombarded by women's energy on the emotional, astral planes.

The Astral emotional process:
All children process their mother's emotional energy from birth to puberty. An emotional umbilical cord automatically attaches itself from the mother to the child when the child is born.

The mother begins to take care of the physical baby and to feed the emotional nourishment to the child's emotional body. This has to be done to keep all of the child's systems working.

The emotional body directly regulates all of the ductless glands, or endocrine system. This system puts out all of our hormones. So the child processes mother's emotional energy until puberty, when they start developing their own emotional body, and the child's own hormonal system kicks in. Then the mother and child go through years of a weaning process.

During the first six months of a male child's life, most of them learn to shut down their solar plexus area. They are receptive, and there is simply too much emotional energy pouring in from mother. It didn't matter if the energy was positive or negative. It was simply too much energy. This early defense patterning, built around their system of survival, is then utilized throughout all of their life, in every emotional encounter they have with women.

Polarity on the mental planes of existence:
Males have a positive polarity on the mental planes. They are more active, larger, and can do more mental labor than females. They are the expressers.
Females have a negative polarity. They are less active, smaller, and can do less mental labor than males. They are the receivers.

The mental plane context is thought and information, structuring time. Females have an easier time taking in information than males do. Little girls have an easier time in school. They can sit still and listen, (take information in) while the little boys are restless and wanting to express-do something.

Polarity on the soul planes of existence:

Males have a negative polarity. They are less active, smaller, and can do less soul labor than females. They are the receivers.

Females have a positive polarity. They are more active, larger, and can do more soul labor than males. They are the expressers.

The soul context is the big picture, the past, spiritual paths and spiritual growth.

Men typically jump to the physical or mental planes, where they are positive, bigger and more capable, when having to deal with emotional or soul issues.

Women typically jump to the emotional or soul planes, where they are positive, bigger and more capable, when having to deal with physical or mental issues.

These four parts of the self, your four bodies, are all connected to each other. They have negative and positive polarities. They interpenetrate and enliven each other. Many times people concentrate on the work that needs to be done in just one of the bodies. They build a big body of experience and expression in either the physical, emotional, mental or soul body. Then the one that has gotten all of the attention and grown so much bigger, begins to think that it runs the show for all of the rest and that it doesn't need the other bodies to live.

Feeding the food each body needs to survive looks like this:

One part of the self, or body cannot live alone. If one dies, they all die. Each part of the self needs a different kind of nourishment to sustain itself. The soul body needs spiritual food and exercise. The mental body needs mental food and exercise. The astral body needs emotional food and exercise. The physical body needs physical food and exercise. Learn to listen to what it is you are hungry for and what part of yourself is asking for it. Take responsibility for that part of the self, define what those needs are for each one, and do something about it on a regular basis.

During the age we are living in right now, the mental body has had more support for growth on planet earth, than all of the other bodies put together. We are just now beginning to understand that for one part of God to exist, all parts have to exist. It is slow going, because developing the different parts of the self requires different tools.

That is because all of the parts of the self, move at different and higher vibrations, and in order to work with them, we need to pay attention to developing new tools.

Here is who the big boss really is!

There is an inborn desire to wake up in every part of life. A desire to achieve more awareness of the world it lives in. To understand and connect with it.

There are many souls sleepwalking in this reality. Their conscious awareness is /sleeping resting in the old two dimensional thinking- which is the limited, ancient logic Aristotle introduced as good-bad, right- wrong, he- she. Opposition and opinion. These souls are not awake to the similarities humankind shares.

In the Eastern philosophies, the energy pours down, bringing Spirit into all the vehicles we occupy.

When you realize that you are a part of a bigger Awakening, your awareness comes in a flash, you experience the quickening realization that your-mother and your-self in all their forms, are human; that both share humanity with all other humans.

An energy process takes place: A wake up cry occurs, releasing your soul energies into a higher vibration when this realization occurs. This happens on the third soul plane, and the sound energies you woke up with your cry release your masculine energies and they attach to your feminine on the 5th Elemental plane of energy. Then together those energies fall, the color and element combinations, at different speeds depending on that combination, down into manifestation on one of the energy planes below.

During this process, the combinations of color-elements- masculine- feminine curls similar to a lotus, a curved molecular structure, into a spiral that connects and intertwines throughout your four bodies and places a permanent resonance throughout your bodies. Other awakened beings can then resonate with your energies.

The Ether/ Akashic Elements Dance:

The spirit body's planes, or areas of energy occupation, correlate with the ether or Akashic Element. This is represented by your second finger on each hand. You know, the one you give the bird with?

This is the arena where Light combines with an Element and produces a combination that will be introduced into your bodies through the Etheric web. Naturally, this area is heavily boundarized by the highest of vibrations. Spirit occupies a place all of the energy bodies we have.

The Akashic element is a cloudy white color. The Akashic element was created first, then the fire element. Then the other three elements from fire on down, using this same process.

Thoreal is the archangel of the ether or Akashic element.

Therefore, the colors are a pass off of excesses of the elements.

The Soul body:

The soul body's planes, or areas of energy occupation, correlate with the fire element and the season of summer. This area is boundarized by Spirit from above its energy area, and the mental body below. The soul's planes of energy lie between those two. Soul planes work with expanding awe, searching out the similarities in everything, rituals, ceremonies, religions, spirituality- developing a larger awareness of Nature- organic spirituality.

The mental body:

The mental body's planes, or areas of energy occupation, correlate with the air element, and its season is fall. The mental planes area is boundarized by the vibrations of the soul body above it, and the emotional/astral body below it. Its energy planes lie between those two. The mental planes work with thinking-theorizing-conceiving-conceptualizing-visualizing-organizing.

The astral/emotional body:

The astral or emotional body's planes of energies correlate to the water element and the spring season. The astral planes area is boundarized by the mental body above it and the physical body below it. It's energy planes manifest between those two. The astral plane works with desire-belief-feeling-imagination.

The physical body:

The physical body's planes of energies correspond to the Earth element, and its season is winter. The physical body's planes of energy respond to and manifest the bodies energies above it/faster in vibration- because the physical body is where the seat of conscious awareness resides. It has the steering wheel, one might say. The physical body is the lowest in vibration of the four bodies, but manifestation of all your bodies take place through its conscious awareness. The physical planes work with doing and action.
All forms are more than one dimensional. Therefore they have more than one charge of electricity-magnetism to them.

I did not go into the more complicated matter of
the causal bodies in this book. That is for a later
book.

READ MORE PATSY STANLEY BOOKS! Many
genres including children's books, picture books,
romances for silver agers, juvenile readers, and
more! Funny illustrations with words of wisdom!

More metaphysical books by Patsy Stanley:

The Elements
The Spiritual Nature of Atomic Structure
Chakras, Meridians, and the Color Energies
The Mental Body
Sound Energies
Shield Energies
All these metaphysical books are available
through all online bookstores including Amazon
and Barnes & Noble.

www.ingramcontent.com/pod-product-compliance
Lightning Source LLC
Chambersburg PA
CBHW050429110726
47899CB00008B/2917